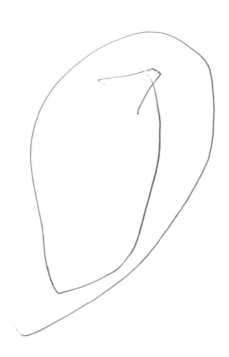

A Beginning-to-Read Book

Dear Dragon Goes to the Hospital

by Margaret Hillert

illustrated by David Schimmell

NORWOOD HOUSE PRESS

DEAR CAREGIVER, The *Beginning-to-Read* series is a carefully written collection of classic readers you may remember from your own childhood. Each book features text comprised of common sight words to provide your child ample practice reading the words that appear most frequently in written text. The many additional details in the pictures enhance the story and offer the opportunity for you to help your child expand oral language and develop comprehension.

Begin by reading the story to your child, followed by letting him or her read familiar words and soon your child will be able to read the story independently. At each step of the way, be sure to praise your reader's efforts to build his or her confidence as an independent reader. Discuss the pictures and encourage your child to make connections between the story and his or her own life. At the end of the story, you will find reading activities and a word list that will help your child practice and strengthen beginning reading skills.

Above all, the most important part of the reading experience is to have fun and enjoy it!

Shannon Cannon

Shannon Cannon, Ph.D.
Literacy Consultant

Norwood House Press • P.O. Box 316598 • Chicago, Illinois 60631
For more information about Norwood House Press please visit our website at
www.norwoodhousepress.com or call 866-565-2900.

Text copyright ©2015 by Margaret Hillert. Illustrations and cover design copyright ©2015 by Norwood House Press, Inc. All rights reserved. No part of this book may be reproduced or utilized in any form or by any means without written permission from the publisher.

LIBRARY OF CONGRESS CATALOGING-IN-PUBLICATION DATA
Hillert, Margaret.
  Dear Dragon goes to the hospital / by Margaret Hillert ; illustrated by David Schimmell.
    pages cm. -- (A beginning-to-read book)
  Summary: "After breaking his leg, a boy and his pet dragon get help at a hospital. Then, they learn new ways to pass time. This title includes reading activities and a word list"-- Provided by publisher.
  ISBN 978-1-59953-581-4 (library edition : alk. paper) -- ISBN 978-1-60357-436-5 (ebook)
  [1. Hospitals--Fiction. 2. Medical care--Fiction. 3. Fractures--Fiction. 4. Dragons--Fiction.] I. Schimmell, David, illustrator. II. Title.
  PZ7.H558Decm 2013
  [E]--dc23
                    2012051133

252N–072014
Manufactured in the United States of America in Stevens Point, Wisconsin.

Let's go!
Let's go, Dear Dragon!
We will have fun!

Oh, oh.
Oh, oh.
O-o-o-o-h!

Uh-oh! I am not good.
Are you alright, Dear Dragon?

Are you two alright?
Can you walk?

No Father, I cannot walk.
This is not good.
Can we do something?

Yes, yes.
We can go to a spot
where we can get help.

Away we go.
Away we go.
We will get help at this hospital.

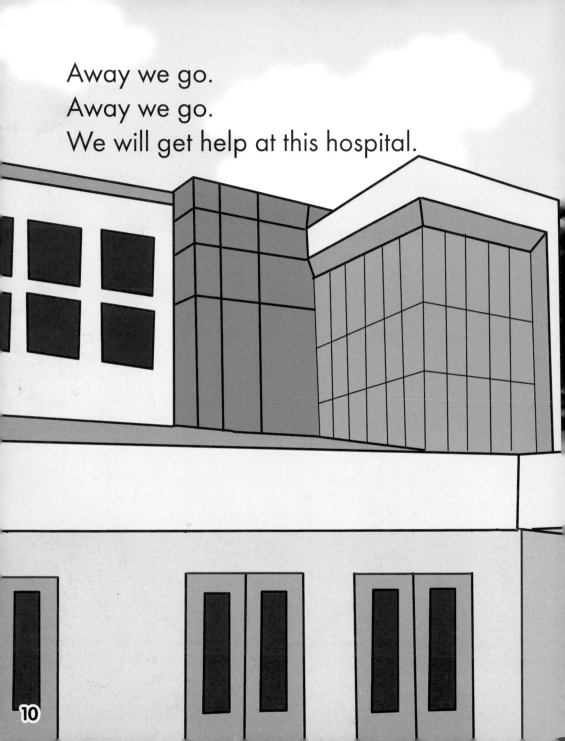

What have we here?
Come in.
Come in.

CHECK-IN

12

Go here.
Go here.
You will see the doctor.

Doctor, can you help
me and my dragon?

This is good.

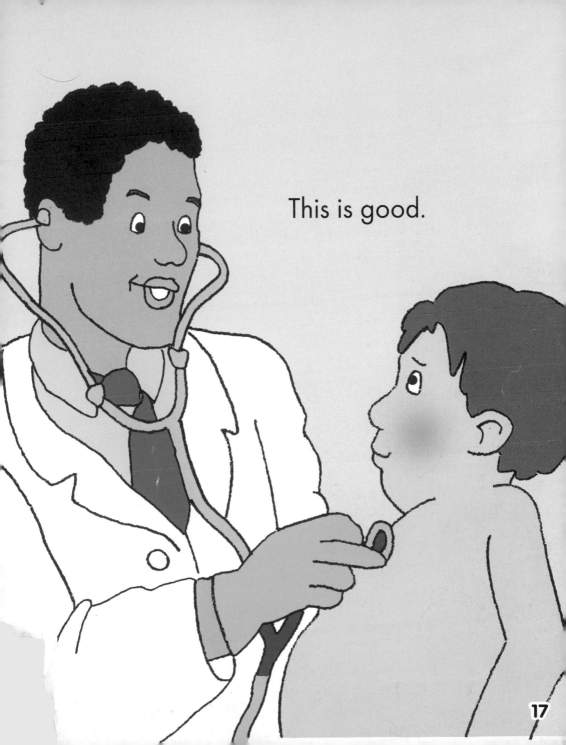

This is good.

But, your leg is not good.
It is broken.

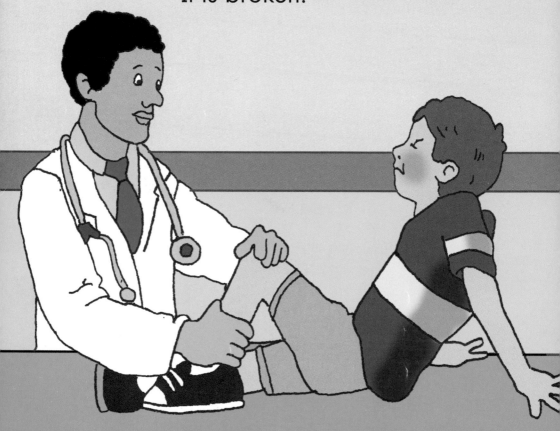

We will do this.

And take these.
It will help.

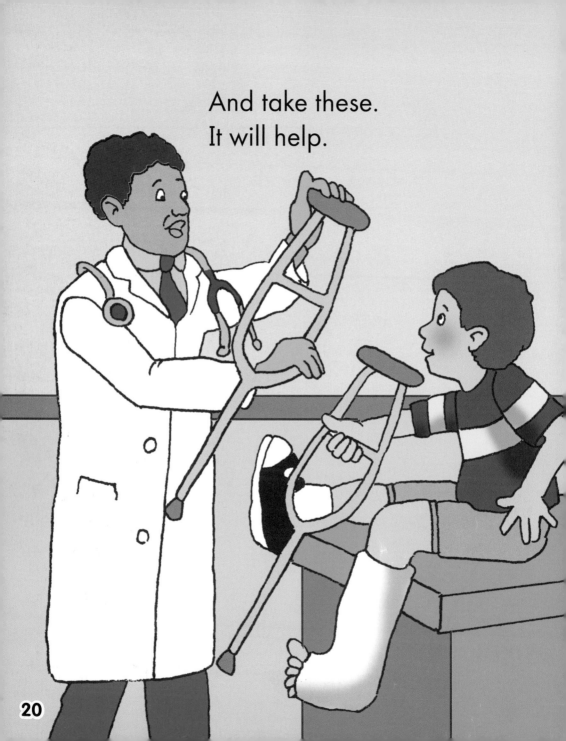

Yes, this will help the dragon.
You and your dragon can
go home and rest.

But what can I do now?
I cannot play with the ball.

I cannot ride this bike.

I cannot put these on.

But we can do this —

and this –

and this.

You are here with me.
My friend is with us, too.
Oh, what a happy day, Dear Dragon.

READING REINFORCEMENT

The following activities support the findings of the National Reading Panel that determined the most effective components for reading instruction are: Phonemic Awareness, Phonics, Vocabulary, Fluency, and Text Comprehension.

Phonemic Awareness: The /h/ sound

Sound Substitution: Say the words on the left to your child. Ask your child to repeat the word, changing the first sound to /h/:

pot - /h/ = hot	sit - /h/ = hit	top - /h/ = hop
ball - /h/ = hall	pat - /h/ = hat	book - /h/ = hook
nose - /h/ = hose	seat - /h/ = heat	jam - /h/ = ham

Phonics: The letter Hh

1. Demonstrate how to form the letters **H** and **h** for your child.

2. Have your child practice writing **H** and **h** at least three times each.

3. Write down the following words on a piece of paper. Ask your child to write the letter **h** in front of them to make a new word:

__air	__and	__eat	__old
__eel	__ear	__is	__ill

4. Read the new words aloud. Ask your child to read all of the words that he or she knows.

Vocabulary: Homophones

1. Find the words *to*, *too*, and *two* in the book. Read the sentences that include each word.

2. Explain to your child that words that sound the same but have different meanings are called homophones.

3. Write each word on a piece of paper. Say sentences including each word and ask your child to point to the correct word for each sentence. For example, which one goes with "I am going (to) the store." Or "There are (two) shoes in a pair."

Fluency: Choral Reading

1. Reread the story with your child at least two more times while your child tracks the print by running a finger under the words as they are read. Ask your child to read the words he or she knows with you.

2. Reread the story aloud together. Be careful to read at a rate that your child can keep up with.

3. Repeat choral reading and allow your child to be the lead reader and ask him or her to change from a whisper to a loud voice while you follow along and change your voice.

Text Comprehension: Discussion Time

1. Ask your child to retell the sequence of events in the story.

2. To check comprehension, ask your child the following questions:

   • Why is the boy unable to walk on page 8?

   • Where did Father take the boy and Dear Dragon to get help?

   • What did the doctor do to help the boy and Dear Dragon feel better?

   • Describe a time when you did not feel well. Who helped you and how?

WORD LIST

Dear Dragon Goes to the Hospital **uses the 71 words listed below.**

The **6** words bolded below serve as an introduction to new vocabulary, while the other 65 are pre-primer. You may wish to write the words on index cards and use them to help your child build automatic word recognition. Regular practice with these words will enhance your child's fluency in reading connected text.

a	do	I	play	uh-oh
alright	**doctor**	in	put	us
am	dragon	is		
and		it	rest	**walk**
are	father		ride	we
at	for	**leg**		what
away	friend	let's		where
	fun	look	see	will
ball			something	with
bike	get	me	spot	
broken	go	my		yes
but	good		take	you
			the	your
can	happy	no	these	
cannot	have	not	this	
come	help	now	to	
	here		too	
day	home	oh	two	
dear	**hospital**	on		

ABOUT THE AUTHOR

Margaret Hillert has written over 80 books for children who are just learning to read. Her books have been translated into many different languages and over a million children throughout the world have read her books. She first started writing poetry as a child and has continued to write for children and adults throughout her life. A first grade teacher for 34 years, Margaret is now retired from teaching and lives in Michigan where she likes to write, take walks in the morning, and care for her three cats.

Photograph by Glenna Washburn

ABOUT THE ILLUSTRATOR

David Schimmell served as a professional firefighter for 23 years before hanging up his boots and helmet to devote himself to working as an illustrator of children's books. David has happily created illustrations for the New Dear Dragon books as well as other artwork for educational and retail book projects. Born and raised in Evansville, Indiana, he lives there today with his wife and family.